# PIZZA!

**First Steck-Vaughn Edition 1992**

Copyright © 1989 American Teacher Publications

Published by Steck-Vaughn Company

Library of Congress number: 89-3623

**Library of Congress Cataloging in Publication Data.**

Martino, Teresa.
  Pizza! / Teresa Martino; illustrated by Brigid Faranda.

  (Real readers)
  Summary: A brief history of pizza as it is now prepared in America, for beginning readers.
  1. Pizza—Juvenile literature. [1. Pizza.] I. Faranda, Brigid, ill. II. Title. III. Series.
TX770.P58M34  1989        641.8′24—dc19        89-3623

ISBN 0-8172-3533-7    hardcover library binding

ISBN 0-8114-6730-9    softcover binding

  3  4  5  6  7  8  9  0    96  95  94  93  92

# PIZZA!

by Teresa Martino
Illustrated by Brigid Faranda

STECK-VAUGHN
C O M P A N Y
A Subsidiary of National Education Corporation

Over 1,000 years ago, people who lived in little towns in Italy baked all their own bread. They did not bake at home. All the people used one big oven. They had to wait a long time for the bread to bake. Sometimes they got hungry.

One day, a woman wanted something to eat while she waited for her bread to bake. She had an idea. She took a bit of bread dough and made it round and flat. Then she put it in the oven. It baked fast.

The woman had something good to eat while she waited for her bread to bake. This was the first pizza.

For many, many years people in Italy made pizza that way. Then they began to add tomatoes and other good things to their pizza. Pizzas changed over the years.

The places people lived in changed, too. Soon towns and cities had lots of different kinds of shops. In Italy, there were some shops that made pizza.

Raffaele Esposito was a pizza baker who had a shop in Naples, Italy, 100 years ago. In some ways, the pizza Raffaele Esposito made then was like the pizza we have now. But in one way, his pizza was different. It did not have any cheese on it.

This is how Mr. Esposito made his pizza. He put red tomatoes on top of flat, round dough. He put on green leaves of basil, too. Basil is a plant that people put in food. It gave the pizza a nice taste.

The people of Naples liked Mr. Esposito's pizzas. Many people said that Raffaele Esposito made the best pizza in all of Italy.

One day, the king of Italy came to see Mr. Esposito. He asked the baker to make a very fine pizza. It was to be for the queen of Italy, Queen Margherita.

Raffaele Esposito was very happy! He was going to make a pizza for the queen!

A pizza for the queen!

The baker wanted to make a new kind of pizza for the queen. He wanted it to taste good. He wanted it to look good, too.

What was the best pizza for the queen of Italy? Mr. Esposito sat down to think about it.

Mr. Esposito looked at the flag of Italy. It had the colors of red, green, and white. The flag gave him an idea. The queen's pizza would have these colors, too!

Mr. Esposito picked the best red tomatoes. He picked the best green basil. But what could he use for the color white?

The baker sat down to think some more.
Soon he had an idea. He could use white
cheese!

Mr. Esposito began to make the queen's pizza. He made the dough round and flat. He put on the best red tomatoes. He put on the best green basil. He put on the best white cheese.

Then he let the pizza bake. When the pizza was done, it looked great!

The queen of Italy ate the pizza. She liked it a lot.

The cheese tasted very good.

Soon, many people wanted pizza with cheese on top. Other pizza shops in Italy began to put cheese on their pizzas, too.

For a long time, people in America did not know about pizza. A man named Gennaro Lombardini changed that.

Mr. Lombardini came from Naples to live in New York City. When he lived in Naples, he had liked to eat pizza. But there was no pizza in New York! So, in 1905 he set up his own pizza shop. His shop was in New York City, but he made pizza with cheese, just the way Raffaele Esposito had made it in Naples, Italy.

Today, bakers everywhere make pizza with cheese on top.

Thank you, Raffaele Esposito!

## Sharing the Joy of Reading

Beginning readers enjoy reading books on their own. Reading a book is a worthwhile activity in and of itself for a young reader. However, a child's reading can be even more rewarding if it is shared. This sharing can enhance your child's appreciation — both of the book and of his or her own abilities.

   Now that your child has read **Pizza!**, you can help extend your child's reading experience by encouraging him or her to:

- Retell the story or key concepts presented in this story in his or her own words. The retelling can be oral or written.

- Create a picture of a favorite character, event, or concept from this book.

- Express his or her own ideas and feelings about the subject of this book and other things he or she might want to know about this subject.

Here is a special activity that you and your child can do together to further extend the appreciation of this book: You and your child can make a pizza. Take a slice of French bread, an English muffin half, or another type of bread. Top the bread with tomatoes or tomato sauce. Add pieces of basil (if you wish) and mozzarella or other cheese. Then pop it in the oven at 350° and bake until the cheese has melted — and VOILA! You have a homemade pizza fit for a queen.